Into My Mother's Arms

Into

Fitzhenry & Whiteside

My Mother's Arms

by Sharon Jennings

Illustrations by Ruth Ohi

Text Copyright © 2000 by Sharon Jennings
Illustrations Copyright © 2000 by Ruth Ohi

First published in the United States in 2000.

Fitzhenry & Whiteside acknowledges with thanks the support
of the Government of Canada through its Book Publishing Industry
Development Program.

Printed in Hong Kong.
Book Design by Wycliffe Smith Design Inc..

10 9 8 7 6 5 4 3 2

Canadian Cataloguing in Publication Data

Jennings, Sharon,
Into my mother's arms

ISBN 1-55041-533-6

I. Ohi, Ruth. II. Title.

PS8569.E563I57 2000   jC813'.54   C99-933106-X
PZ7.J46In 2000

To the Meloshe family, with thanks.

Sharon

For my Sara.

R.O.

When morning comes,
I lie down beside my mother
until she wakes up.

She likes that.

6

I lead the way downstairs for breakfast.
I pour the cereal and my mother
pours the milk. I tell her
what I want to be
when I'm big.

Soon my mother says
we have work to do.
I help make our beds,
and …

when the mail arrives, I open all the envelopes.

When we go out,
I tell my mother to wear
the yellow dress. The yellow dress
makes her look like sunshine.

I wear my yellow dress too.

At the store, I show
my mother where
everything is.
She always forgets
and I always
remember.

16

But I can't
remember
if we have
cookies at
home.

My mother
buys the kind
I like best,
just in case.

My mother says that we can
stop at the park.

I think that this time I will go
down the big slide.

At the top
I change my mind.

But someone is
waiting behind me.

I see my mother at the bottom,
and she smiles at me.

And I slide
down and
down…

22

and into my mother's arms.

We lie in the grass
and make angels. My mother wears
the dandelion crown I make her.

At home we put away
the groceries.

My mother makes tea and I bring her
my book. I sit in her lap, and I am not afraid
when we read about the dragon.

After dinner,
it is time
for my bath.

I use my mother's
soap, and I smell
just like her.

28

I tell my mother I want to be like her
when I grow up.

When bedtime comes, my mother
lies down beside me…

...until I fall asleep.

I like that.